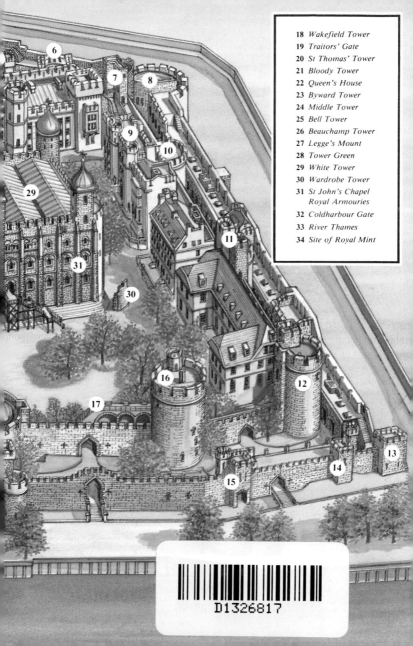

For nine centuries the Tower has kept watch over the City of London and the River Thames. The fascinating history of this former palace, fortress and prison, and the story of the people who have lived within its walls, are told in this book.

Acknowledgments:
The publishers and the author (Education Officer at the Tower of London) would like to thank the staff at the Royal Armouries for their help and advice, and the following for permission to use illustrative material:
Ashmolean Museum, page 17 (bottom); British Library, pages 7 (top left), 10, 11 (top); Tim Clark, photographs on pages 11, 12 (bottom) and 27 (top); Department of the Environment (Crown copyright), front and back covers, title page, and pages 4, 5 (bottom), 9, 14 (top), 15, 16 (bottom and bottom inset), 17 (top), 18, 19 (top), 20, 21 (bottom), 22, 24, 25, 26 (top), 28 (top), 31, 32, 33, 42 (bottom), 46, 47 (top and bottom), 48, 49; Fotomas Index, pages 21 (top), 30 (bottom), 35 (top); Maltings Design Partnership, illustrations on front endpaper and pages 6/7, 8, 12, 26/7, 35, 37, 42/3, 50/51; Anne Matthews, line drawing on page 29 (bottom); Museum of London, page 5 (top); National Portrait Gallery, pages 20 (inset), 23, 42, 43, 45; Public Record Office, page 19 (bottom right); by permission of H M Queen, pages 23 (top left), 28 (bottom); Royal Armouries Board of Trustees, pages 13, 15 (inset), 16 (inset), 19 (bottom left), 29 (inset), 34, 36, 38, 39, 40, 40/41, 47 (middle); Royal Holloway College, page 44; Society of Antiquaries, page 14 (bottom); Syndication International, page 30 (top).
Designed by Graham Marlow and Chris Reed.

British Library Cataloguing in Publication Data

Hammond, Peter, *1937-*
    Discovering the Tower of London.—(Discovering).
    1. Tower of London—Guide-books—Juvenile literature
    2. London (England)—Castles—Juvenile literature
    I. Title
    914.21′5   DA687.T7

    ISBN 0-7214-1002-2

First edition

Published by Ladybird Books Ltd Loughborough Leicestershire UK
Ladybird Books Inc Lewiston Maine 04240 USA

© LADYBIRD BOOKS LTD MCMLXXXVII

Printed in England

DISCOVERING
The Tower
of London

written by
PETER HAMMOND

Ladybird Books

The Tower of London from the air

The Tower of London

The Tower of London was begun by William the Conqueror as a fortress and palace. Later kings made it larger and stronger, and kept soldiers, armour, weapons, treasure, and sometimes important prisoners there. For five hundred years coins of the realm were minted at the Tower and official documents stored in some of the castle buildings. There was even a zoo there which began as the king's private collection of animals.

It was not until after 1850 that the Tower became, first and foremost, a tourist attraction and even today many people live and work there, sometimes perhaps joined by the ghosts from the Tower's long and eventful past.

For nine centuries the Tower has kept watch over London and the River Thames. For more than five hundred years the Tower stood on the very edge of London, for it was not until Tudor times that London began to spread rapidly beyond the city walls.

The Great Fire of London, 1666 – an eyewitness view. The Tower only just escaped when the wind changed, blowing the flames back into the city

Until the building of the London docks, early in the nineteenth century, hundreds of merchant ships lay at anchor between the Tower and London Bridge.

Ships in the Pool of London, 1804

Fortress and Palace *The beginning of the Tower*

In 1066 William, Duke of Normandy, and his men
defeated the Saxons at the Battle of Hastings and killed
the Saxon king, Harold. William and the Normans then
set about building castles to complete their domination
of England. One of the earliest castles was built where
the Tower now stands. It was simply a timber fort,
erected in a corner of the stone walls which the Romans
had built around their city of London nine hundred
years before.

In 1078 William the Conqueror ordered work to begin
on a much grander castle, a great tower of stone, which
would guard London and also show off his power and
wealth. The walls of William's Tower stand 90 feet

*The building of the White Tower took about twenty years.
Immense quantities of stone had to be brought from quarries, then
shaped and put in place. Once the stone and timber had been
carried to the site in carts or in boats, all the work had to be done
by hand (or even by foot if treadwheels were used).*

Cut stones called ashlar, *which fitted together exactly, were used
to strengthen the corners and window openings, but the walls of
the White Tower were mainly built of rubble – pieces of stone set
in cement*

(27.3 m) high and are 15 feet (4.6 m) thick at the base. Most of the stone was brought by river from Kent, though some was even shipped across the Channel from Normandy.

A thirteenth century drawing showing a king giving orders to his architect and builders working

There was only one doorway, still in use today, set high above the ground and out of reach of battering ram and fire. The window openings were once much smaller, especially near to the ground, again for security. A few of the original windows remain, on the top storey over the entrance. To make this great tower even more impressive the walls were whitewashed and so it got its name – **the White Tower**.

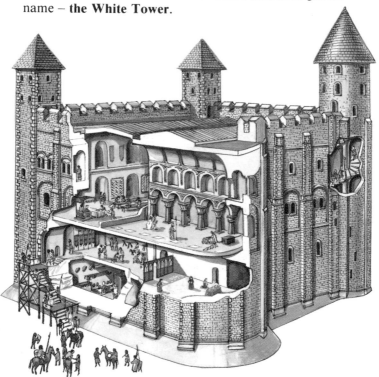

This is perhaps how the White Tower would have looked inside when kings stayed there in medieval times. The king's chair is under a canopy in the great hall, on the top floor. Next to it is St John's Chapel. Notice the gallery which overlooks these grand rooms. Much later, another floor was put in at the level of the gallery

Since Tudor times the White Tower has been filled with armour and weapons, but once it contained a royal palace, as well as being the residence of the Constable who commanded the Tower for the king. The Constable's rooms were on the entrance floor, and the king's great hall, apartments and chapel were on the floor above. In most of the rooms only a few features are left from those days – fireplaces, some of the lavatories (called 'garderobes'), and a well in the basement – but **St John's Chapel** has scarcely changed for nine hundred years. Here it is not hard to imagine a Norman king at prayer, with his barons and his knights.

St John's Chapel today

The Welsh prince, Gruffyd, falls from the top of the White Tower

Strangely enough, the first person to live in the palace in the White Tower, in 1100, was not a king but a prisoner, named Ranulf Flambard. He soon escaped down a rope from an upper window.

In 1244 a Welsh prince, Gruffyd, tried to do the same. But his rope was made of knotted bedsheets which came apart and Gruffyd fell to his death. In 1358 King John of France and his son, who had been captured in battle, were held in the White Tower for a time. Once, even an English king, Richard II, was held prisoner there; Richard was forced to give up his crown to his cousin, Henry Bolingbroke, who became Henry IV.

King Richard II hands over the Crown and Sceptre to the new king, his cousin, Henry IV

The basement rooms in the White Tower are often called the dungeons. Sometimes prisoners were kept there, and perhaps even tortured. But usually these rooms were filled with stores of food and weapons.

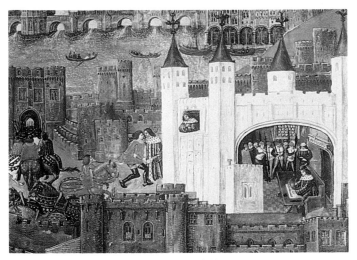

The Tower and City of London, about 1490

The expansion of the Tower

As London grew, its citizens wanted more freedom and less taxation. So, to keep the rebellious Londoners in order, the Tower of London was developed into one of the greatest castles in Britain.

Beginning in the reign of Richard the Lionheart, a hundred years after the time of William the Conqueror, a line of walls and towers was built around the White Tower. Beginning in 1275, during the reign of King Edward I, a second line of defences was built and surrounded with a great moat.

The Beauchamp Tower was built by Edward I, as well as the walls beside it and in front

Edward I had been to the Holy Land on a crusade before he became king, and in his travels he had seen all the latest ideas in castle building. After completing the expansion of the Tower, Edward went on to build great castles like Caernarfon and Conwy during his conquest of Wales.

It would have been almost impossible for an enemy army to fight their way into the Tower. They could only cross the moat along a causeway guarded by three towers, one behind the other, equipped with

The Middle Tower and the Byward Tower guarded the causeway across the moat

12

This windlass raised and lowered the portcullis at the Byward Tower

drawbridges, gates, portcullises and murder-holes. As the attackers tried to pass each of these obstacles they would have been showered with arrows and stones from the battlements and arrow slits nearby. The other entrance to the Tower was even harder to break through because it led directly from the River Thames, through the watergate that later came to be called **Traitors' Gate**.

Even when great guns were made that could break down the strongest walls, the Tower was still a formidable fortress, with its own guns pointing across the river and over London. It also had a large garrison of soldiers. The vast **Waterloo Barracks**, housing one thousand men, were built in the nineteenth century, when the Duke of Wellington was Constable of the Tower.

Legge's Mount, one of two gun emplacements overlooking Tower Hill

The palace in the Tower

During the reign of Edward I's father, Henry III, a new palace took shape between the White Tower and the river. There was a great hall and, next to it, the royal apartments. These were comfortable and richly decorated rooms with large windows to give plenty of light, and hooded fireplaces, to take out the smoke – very different from the dark, draughty rooms in the White Tower. Here, in the palace, kings held council and royal babies were born. Nearby, in the towers along the castle walls, important officials and the king's guests had their own rooms or sets of rooms.

The remains of the wall painting in the Byward Tower dating from about 1400

On the eve of a coronation the new monarch feasted in the great hall, and there, the next day, he knighted the young noblemen who had kept vigil all night in St John's Chapel. Then, in a great procession, he rode out from the Tower through cheering crowds to be crowned in Westminster Abbey.

The nine year old Edward VI goes to his coronation from the Tower

Henry VIII and Queen's House, built in his reign

The last king to spend much time at the Tower was
Henry VIII. He later moved to more splendid palaces,
like Hampton Court and Whitehall. The palace buildings
began to fall into decay and were eventually pulled
down. Even so, the Tower is still known as a royal
palace. On the turrets of the White Tower are wind
vanes painted with the royal arms, with crowns above
them, and soldiers still mount guard at the Tower, as
they do at Buckingham Palace.

The Changing of the Guard in front of Queen's House

The zoo, mint and record office

The palace at the Tower had its own zoo. It began when Henry III was given three leopards by the German Emperor, a polar bear by the King of Norway, and an elephant by the King of France. The bear was allowed to go fishing in the Thames, at the end of a strong rope. A house was built for the elephant which died after two years. Soon it became a tradition that there should always be lions at the Tower, for heraldic lions appear in the royal arms of England.

Eventually, there was not enough space for the animals which were by then kept at the main entrance to the Tower, in the **Lion Tower** (later pulled down).

In 1834 the Tower zoo was closed, and some of the animals were sent to the new London zoo in Regent's Park.

The Lions' den in the old zoo in the Lion Tower. The admission ticket for the 'Washing of the Lions' is a joke!

TOWER OF LONDON.

Admit the Bearer and Friends
TO VIEW THE
ANNUAL CEREMONY
OF
WASHING THE LIONS,
ON MONDAY, APRIL THE 1st, 1856.

Herbert de Grafse
Senior Warden.

ADMITTED ONLY AT THE WHITE GATE.

It is requested that no Gratuities will be given to the Wardens on any account.

Here is Marco, one of many lions who once lived in the Tower zoo

16

A mint at work around 1500

The mint had been moved into the Tower for safety by the reign of Edward I and stayed there until 1811. For most of that time the coins were made by hand. Later, hand-operated presses were used.

The mint buildings were between the inner and outer walls of the Tower. The present day Royal Mint is at Llantrisant in Wales.

A gold sovereign from the reign of Henry VII, made at the Tower

front

back

For almost six hundred years, the Tower housed an ever-growing collection of official documents consisting of the records kept by lawcourts and government departments. Eventually, the **Wakefield Tower** and part of the White Tower, including St John's Chapel, were filled with these public records. They were moved out in the 1850s, after a new Public Record Office had been built in Chancery Lane, London.

The prison

The Tower became famous, and feared, as a prison during the troubled times of the Tudors and Stuarts. Those who disagreed with the ruler of the day, if they were dangerous or important enough, were likely to be sent to the Tower as traitors. If the prisoner had taken part in a plot or rebellion he might be tortured, to make him confess and name others involved.

Traitors' Gate. Prisoners were admitted here

The forms of torture used at the Tower were the rack, which painfully stretched out the prisoner's joints; the 'Scavenger's Daughter' which squeezed the prisoner tighter and tighter; and the manacles – iron bands from which the prisoner hung by the wrists. He might also be put into a horribly tiny cell called 'Little Ease' or into 'the dungeon with the rats'. Exactly where these evil cells were situated is not known.

A Tower prisoner, Cuthbert Simpson, being tortured in the 'Scavenger's Daughter' and on the rack. The 'Scavenger's Daughter' (below left) can be seen today in the Bowyer Tower

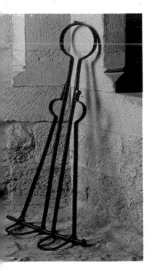

When Guy Fawkes was taken off the rack, he could only scrawl his first name on his confession. Later, he was able to sign a second confession properly, but his hand was still shaky

Sir Thomas More and his prison, the Bell Tower

Not all prisoners who were awaiting trial were so badly
treated, but they would be kept in solitary confinement
and might be left without proper food, clothing and
warmth. Sir Thomas More, for example, had been King
Henry VIII's Chancellor and friend. But when Sir
Thomas would not accept Henry as Head of the Church
instead of the Pope, he was kept for fifteen months as a
'close prisoner' in a cold bare room in the **Bell Tower**,
cut off from his family and friends. Even then, however,
he would not say what the king wanted to hear and was
charged with treason.

Sir Thomas More died by the axe just outside the Tower on **Tower Hill**, where over a hundred other Tower prisoners were beheaded, most of them in Tudor times. These executions were public, watched by thousands of people who mostly came for the excitement. Today, the block used at the last beheading on Tower Hill in 1747 is kept in the **Bowyer Tower**, along with an axe of the Tudor period, and some of the torture instruments.

The Earle of Strafford for treasonable practises beheaded on the Tower-hill

In 1641 the beheading of Strafford, Charles I's chief minister, was watched by 100,000 people

The block on show at the Tower was made taller than usual for the eighty year old Lord Lovat, so that he could kneel upright and would only have to bend his neck. Previous blocks were so low that the prisoner had to lie full length

Seven prisoners were beheaded inside the Tower walls, on **Tower Green**. Five were women, including two of Henry VIII's six wives, Anne Boleyn and Catherine Howard. When Henry allowed Anne to choose how she would die she asked for a very sharp sword instead of the axe. A headsman was specially brought over from France where this was then the method of beheading.

The bodies of those who died on the Green, as well as most of the prisoners beheaded on Tower Hill, were buried in **St Peter's Chapel** on the Green. St Peter's has always been the Tower's parish church as well. Not only prisoners but many who lived and worked in the Tower were buried there and it is still used for christenings and weddings in Yeoman Warders' families, as well as for regular Sunday services.

St Peter's Chapel

Some prisoners of the Tower

Not even the highest in the land were safe from imprisonment or execution

1 *The future Elizabeth I was held prisoner in the Tower when she was just twenty years old. She was accused of plotting against her half-sister, Queen Mary I*

2 *Anne Boleyn, Henry VIII's second wife and mother of Elizabeth I, was beheaded for treason*

3 *Lady Jane Grey was executed at the age of sixteen. She had been Queen of England for nine days*

4 *Thomas Cromwell, Henry VIII's chief minister, executed in 1540*

5 *Robert Devereux, second Earl of Essex, one time favourite of Elizabeth I, eventually lost his life on the executioner's block*

6 *Thomas Cranmer, Archbishop of Canterbury under Henry VIII, imprisoned in the Tower and later burned at the stake*

Death by beheading was considered a privilege, allowed only to prisoners of noble birth. Other traitors died a still more horrible death, after being dragged across London on a hurdle to Tyburn, near Marble Arch. Here they were hanged, drawn, and quartered, before their remains were put on show as a terrible warning.

Some prisoners were spared execution, but remained in the Tower for many years. Some were still 'close prisoners' but others had the 'liberty of the Tower', meaning that during the day they were allowed out to take exercise and perhaps visit other prisoners. They might even have an entire tower for themselves, their family, and servants. Sir Walter Raleigh was a prisoner for twelve years in the **Bloody Tower** where he wrote a lengthy *History of the World*.

Sir Walter Raleigh and one of the rooms in the Bloody Tower where he was imprisoned

The Beauchamp Tower and two inscriptions by prisoners on its walls. These remind us of Lady Jane Grey, and the Dudley family who tried to make her Queen in place of Mary Tudor

Many prisoners used up the long and empty hours by cutting inscriptions in the walls of their rooms. In the **Beauchamp Tower** there are almost a hundred inscriptions, some of them connected with Lady Jane Grey, the 'Nine Days Queen'. Her young husband, Guildford Dudley, was locked up there with his father, the Duke of Northumberland, and his brothers. One of the brothers hired a professional stone carver to produce an elaborate family memorial with stone flowers representing their names. Perhaps it was Guildford Dudley who twice scratched Jane's name into the wall.

25

Hugh Draper's astrological chart

In the **Salt Tower** an astrologer, Hugh Draper, carved a chart and a globe. Perhaps he used them to tell the fortunes of his gaolers. There are also religious inscriptions carved by Catholic priests imprisoned there during the reign of the Protestant Queen Elizabeth I.

One of them, John Gerard, managed to escape with the help of friends. His gaoler, who was perhaps secretly a Catholic, allowed him to visit another Catholic prisoner

1 *Gerard and Arden signal from the Cradle Tower to their friends across the moat*

2 *Gerard throws down a cord of bailing twine attached to an iron ball*

3 *The rescuers attach the cord to a length of rope tied to a stake*

4 *Gerard draws up the rope and passes it around a big gun on the tower roof*

1

2

3

The Cradle Tower

in the nearby **Cradle Tower**, overlooking the river, and to send messages to his friends. One night Gerard's friends came by boat and got a rope up to the top of the Cradle Tower down which the two prisoners climbed.

Most of the many hundreds of Tower prisoners, however, did not escape; nor were they tortured, executed, or left in the Tower to die. Instead, after a short while, they were set free.

5 *Arden begins to slide down the rope*

6 *Gerard struggles across the rope towards the wall on the far side of the moat*

7 *The two escaped prisoners are carried off in a rowing boat under cover of darkness*

6

4 5 7

27

The Crown Jewels

The Martin Tower

After the Civil War, and the execution of Charles I in 1649, England had no monarch, so all the Crown Jewels were brought to the Tower to be broken up and sold off. A few pieces were saved though, and reappeared eleven years later when new coronation regalia were made for Charles II. Most of these have been used in coronations ever since.

After Charles II had been crowned the regalia were kept in the **Martin Tower,** and if visitors paid the jewel keeper, they were able to handle them behind locked

Charles II

doors. A daring adventurer, 'Colonel' Thomas Blood, saw his chance. First he won the trust of the keeper, Talbot Edwards, and his family. Then one day, Blood came back with three friends and asked Edwards to show them the jewels. As soon as Edwards had brought them out Blood and his friends knocked him down, and bound and gagged him. Then, with a crown, orb and sceptre hidden in their clothes they hurried out of the Tower.

When they were challenged, Blood shot a guard with his pistol, but then he and two of his accomplices were overpowered and dragged back into the Tower to await punishment (the third man escaped). Curiously, after a private meeting with King Charles, Blood was set free, along with his friends. Perhaps Charles thought it all a great joke, or perhaps Blood knew something that the king wanted kept secret.

Thomas Blood organised the stealing of the Crown Jewels from the Martin Tower. This reconstruction of the scene shows Blood (also shown in the inset) and his friends making their escape, leaving the jewel keeper unconscious on the floor

29

Queen Elizabeth II wears the Imperial State Crown after her coronation in 1953

Easily the most spectacular of the Crown Jewels are the crowns. The oldest and heaviest, St Edward's Crown, is worn by the monarch only at his or her coronation. Although it was made for Charles II in 1661, the lower half may indeed be the crown of the saintly King Edward the Confessor who died in 1066, when the Tower's story begins.

The Bayeux Tapestry showing the crowning of King Harold with the original St Edward's Crown

St Edward's Crown, with which the sovereign is crowned

The Imperial State Crown

The Imperial State Crown is seen much more frequently, because it is worn by the monarch for state occasions like the State Opening of Parliament. It was made for Queen Victoria in 1837, but it is set with famous gems which have been among the Crown Jewels for centuries. The sapphire in the cross at the top may have come from a ring worn by Edward the Confessor. The balas ruby in the front was given to the Black Prince, Edward III's great warrior son, in 1367, and three of the hanging pearls may have belonged to Mary Queen of Scots and then to Elizabeth I. Queen Victoria found even the State Crown too heavy, and a little diamond crown – which can be seen on stamps and coins – was made for her to wear on the top of her head, over her hair which was coiled in a bun.

Queen Victoria's small crown

31

The Crown of Queen Elizabeth, the Queen Mother

The Crown of Queen Elizabeth the Queen Mother contains the Koh-i-noor diamond (the name means 'mountain of light') which was brought from India and given to Queen Victoria. Because of a legend that the Koh-i-noor had always brought bad luck to the men who wore it, it has never been set in the crown of a British king or prince.

The finest gemstone of all among the Crown Jewels is the Star of Africa in the head of the Sceptre with the Cross. It is the largest cut diamond in the world. The second largest appears in the front of the Imperial State Crown. Both were cut from the Cullinan diamond which was found in South Africa in 1905, as well as seven other large stones and ninety six small ones.

The Sceptre with the Cross

The Star of Africa

As well as the coronation regalia and robes, the **Jewel House** at the Tower also contains the silver-gilt dishes and vessels used for coronation banquets and services, ceremonial maces and trumpets for state processions,

The Sovereign's and Queen Mary's Orbs

robes and badges of the orders of knighthood, and medals.

The Prince of Wales Crown, made for Prince George, the future King George V

Charles II salt cellar

Coronation rings (below)

The Cannon Room in the basement of the White Tower

The Royal Armouries

At first the Tower stored only the armour and weapons of the soldiers who guarded it. Then it became the main arsenal in the country, supplying all the royal armies and fleets. As armour and weapons were sent back to the Tower because they were out of date, a museum collection took shape. In the reign of Charles II, more than three hundred years ago, the collection was put on show, making the **Royal Armouries** Britain's oldest public museum.

Armour for man and horse, made for the young Henry VIII

*Norman knights
from the Bayeux Tapestry*

The present day collections of the Royal Armouries display European arms and armour from the age of the Saxons and Vikings up to the First World War, as well as weapons and armour from Asia and Africa.

The first soldiers at the Tower, in Norman times, wore armour of mail, made up of interlinked iron rings. By about 1300 some knights wore shaped plates of iron, on top of the mail, on their legs, arms and bodies. By about 1400 these plates were combined to make up a complete suit of armour.

An armour was made from wrought iron or steel. Using patterns like a dressmaker's, the armourer cut out pieces and hammered them into shape to fit around the body

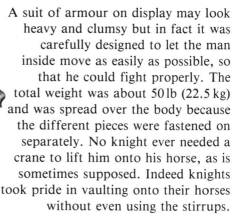

A suit of armour on display may look heavy and clumsy but in fact it was carefully designed to let the man inside move as easily as possible, so that he could fight properly. The total weight was about 50 lb (22.5 kg) and was spread over the body because the different pieces were fastened on separately. No knight ever needed a crane to lift him onto his horse, as is sometimes supposed. Indeed knights took pride in vaulting onto their horses without even using the stirrups.

The best armour was styled according to the fashion of the day, and was 'made to measure'. In the Royal Armouries there are armours for a giant, 6 ft 10 in (2.08 m) tall, and for a dwarf, 3 ft 1½ in (0.95 m) tall. Horses too wore matching armour, if their riders could afford it.

From about 1520 guns became more powerful, because of better gunpowder. Armour was made stronger, but

this made it heavier and more uncomfortable. Soldiers began to leave off arm and leg pieces so that they could move more quickly, and by about 1650, at the end of the Civil War, they often chose to wear no armour at all.

Soldiers of the English Civil War

ARMOUR OF HENRY VIII – 1540

A complete armour was made up of about twenty pieces which were put on separately. Most of the pieces, in turn, were made up of smaller plates fastened together. Although there might be as many as two hundred plates in an armour, it only took about five minutes to put a man into it

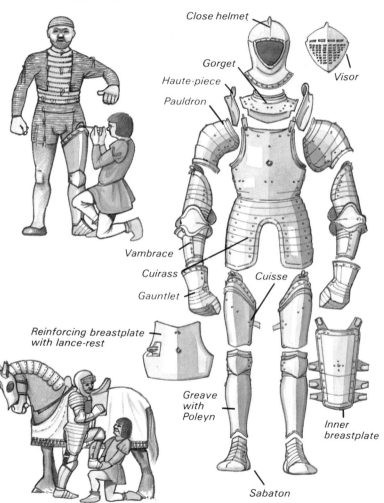

Close helmet

Visor

Gorget

Haute-piece

Pauldron

Vambrace

Cuirass

Gauntlet

Cuisse

Reinforcing breastplate with lance-rest

Greave with Poleyn

Inner breastplate

Sabaton

Armour was also made specially for the mock combats of the tournaments. The most dangerous of these was the joust, when two riders charged against each other with lances. Henry VIII was twice nearly killed while jousting, though his armourers had taken good care to make his armour as strong as

A jousting helmet

possible. When Henry fought in the foot tournament his armour, as well as being strong, had to allow him to move easily and comfortably. As he grew fatter each new armour had to be made bulkier than the last.

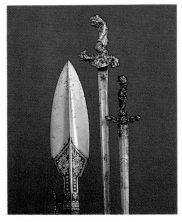

Henry VIII's 1540 armour

Richly decorated hunting weapons

38

This Spanish grandee, the Duke of Alba, chose to be portrayed in a splendid armour he had worn in battle

Tournament armours were often decorated with gold and silver to make a good show. There were even fantastic parade armours meant only for processions to and from the tournament ground, not for the actual combat.

The other great warlike sport was hunting, and swords, crossbows and guns were made specially for use in the hunt. Many of those on display at the Tower are so elaborately decorated they are works of art, probably too precious to have ever been used.

A flintlock pistol, decorated with silver and gold, probably made for King William III ▼

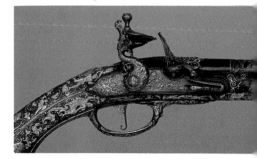

The designs on the wooden stock of this sporting gun are made of staghorn

Japanese Samurai armours: the amazing helmet crests and face masks were meant to impress and frighten the enemy

The armours worn by Asian warriors were made for different climates and different kinds of fighting from those in Europe. They may not look as strong but they were just as well designed. In Japan, Samurai warriors wore some mail and plate but most of their armour was made up of strips of rawhide or steel which were laced together. This light and flexible armour was especially suitable for combat with swords. It allowed the warriors to move quickly, and yet could take blows from the strongest and sharpest swords ever produced.

The armourers of Turkey, Persia and India used mail and plate but put them together differently from the Europeans. The Indian elephant armour at the Tower – the largest armour in the world – is made up of thousands of small plates of iron linked together with mail.

The Turks were the supreme gunfounders of Asia. In the Tower grounds there are several splendid Turkish bronze cannon. One is covered all over with a design of pomegranates and tulips. Another is the great Dardanelles gun which had to be made and carried in two parts. One had to be screwed into the other before the gun could be fired; together they weigh seventeen tons.

The Turkish Dardanelles gun could shoot a cannon ball weighing six hundredweight (about 300 kg) more than a mile

Mysteries and legends

At first the Tower was chiefly famous as an ancient and mighty fortress. It was said that Julius Caesar had begun it, and that the blood of wild animals had been mixed into the mortar that held the stones together. Then, after the Wars of the Roses, stories began of mysterious disappearances and deaths.

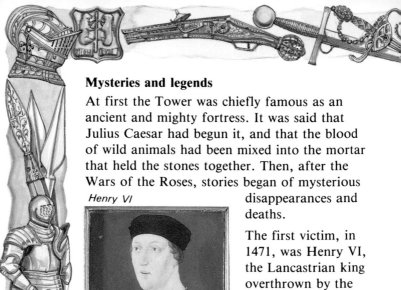

Henry VI

The first victim, in 1471, was Henry VI, the Lancastrian king overthrown by the Yorkist Edward IV. No one believed the official story that Henry had died of grief, and in fact when his skull was examined some years ago it showed that he probably died from a blow on the head. It is said that he was murdered while praying in the Wakefield Tower.

The Wakefield Tower

Edward IV had his own brother put to death in the Tower, as well as his rival, Henry VI

In 1478 Edward IV's brother, George, Duke of Clarence was found guilty of plotting against him, and was privately executed in the Tower. One story at the time was that he chose to die by drowning in a barrel of his favourite wine in the Bowyer Tower.

When Edward IV died in 1483 his two sons were brought to the Tower by their uncle Richard, Duke of Gloucester. The older boy was to be the new king. But then Richard took the crown for himself as Richard III, and the two boys remained in the Tower under guard.

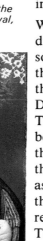

Richard III

The Princes in the Tower, as imagined by the nineteenth century painter, Millais

After a few months they were never seen again. Ever since, there has been argument about what happened to the Princes in the Tower. Perhaps the best known story is that they were murdered in the Bloody Tower. They are said to have been smothered with their own pillows, by order of Richard III, but there is no proof of this. Others beside Richard wished to be king and might have wanted the princes out of the way. One was the Duke of Buckingham, later executed himself by Richard. The other was Henry Tudor, Henry VIII's father, who won the crown at the Battle of Bosworth, where Richard was killed.

In 1674 the bones of two children were found near the White Tower. At the time they were thought to be the princes, but modern experts cannot be sure that the children were boys, let alone the princes, and can find no clue in the bones as to how and when they died.

The last of the Yorkists, the daughter of the Duke of Clarence, suffered a horrible death in the Tower. She was Margaret, Countess of Salisbury. Her brother had been beheaded by order of Henry VII but she became governess to Henry VIII's daughter, Mary. Later her sons were accused of plotting against the king, and the Countess, by now in her seventies, was brought to the Tower.

Henry VII, the first Tudor king

Two years later the Countess was beheaded, but not with a single stroke of the axe as was usual. The Countess would not lie still with her head on the block, and it took several blows of the axe before she was finally beheaded.

Since so many people suffered and even died within the walls, it is not surprising that the Tower has more ghost stories than any other place in Britain. The figures of many famous prisoners have been seen, including Henry VI and the two princes, and there have been many reports of strange shapes, phantom footsteps and invisible presences. Perhaps the ghost most often seen is Anne Boleyn's, which walks in front of **Queen's House** where it is said she was a prisoner before her execution on Tower Green.

Margaret Pole, Countess of Salisbury, a Yorkist put to death by the Tudor Henry VIII

45

Tower Green, showing Queen's House

Behind the scenes

Even when it is busy with thousands of visitors the Tower carries on with its own life. It is home for about one hundred and fifty people, including the Tower officers, the Yeoman Warders and their families. In fact the Tower is rather like the traditional English village with its squire, the Resident Governor, in the Queen's House, and its doctor and parson, while the recreation ground is the Tower moat.

The ravens are certainly among the most important residents in the Tower, for – so the story goes – if they ever leave, the Tower will fall and England with it. As soon as the castle was built ravens must have flown in to feed off the

The Chief Yeoman Warder with his mace of office

rubbish from the kitchens and there may have been some at the Tower ever since.

These days there are usually about six ravens hopping and pecking around the Tower lawns in the daytime. They are cared for by one of the Yeoman Warders, who feeds them on raw meat, biscuit soaked in blood, rabbits' heads, fruit and eggs. He talks them back into their cage every night, and from time to time clips their wings – just to make sure that they never do leave.

As well as tourists, many thousands of schoolchildren and students come to the Tower each year on educational visits. For them there is a specially equipped education centre, with filmshows, lessons, and the chance to handle historic armour, costume and even the Crown Jewels – in replica. Work also goes on behind the scenes to discover more about the Tower's past and to restore more of the buildings to their original appearance, so that they can be put on show to the public.

The Yeoman Ravenmaster in everyday uniform

King or Queen for a day!

Archaeologists at work at the Tower

Yeoman Warders in state dress

Traditions and ceremonies

Just as in the time of William the Conqueror, the Tower is commanded for the monarch by the Constable, but nowadays the Resident Governor in Queen's House is in day-to-day charge and commands the Body of Yeoman Warders of the Tower.

The Yeoman Warders have guarded the Tower since the reign of Henry VIII. They are often called 'Beefeaters', but that name really belongs to the Yeomen of the Guard, who are the personal escort of the sovereign and who used to be given extra rations of beef to keep them strong.

At present there are about forty Yeoman Warders at the Tower. They are former warrant officers who have served in the Army, Royal Air Force or Royal Marines, for at least twenty two years. Usually they wear the dark blue and red uniform. For state occasions like the sovereign's birthday or the opening of Parliament, the Yeoman Warders, like the Yeomen of the Guard on duty at the Tower, wear Tudor bonnets and scarlet and gold tunics, the picturesque state dress for which they are famous throughout the world.

A gun salute fired from Tower Wharf

State occasions are also marked by the firing of a gun salute, from the **Tower Wharf,** by the Honourable Artillery Company. Sixty two guns are fired for the anniversary of the sovereign's birthday, accession and coronation, and forty one guns on other state occasions.

Every day at the Tower ends with the Ceremony of the Keys. The soldiers of the Tower Guard escort the Chief Yeoman Warder as he locks the outer gates. When this is done the guard salute 'the Queen's keys' and the Chief Warder calls out 'God preserve Queen Elizabeth.' Then he takes the keys to the Governor in Queen's House. The Tower of London is safe and secure for the night.

The Ceremony of the Keys, when the Tower is locked up for the night

Tower timeline

1100

The great palace-fortress, later called the White Tower, was built for William the Conqueror, to keep guard over London and its river, and to show off the power of the Norman kings

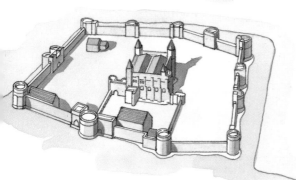

1272

By the end of Henry III's reign, the White Tower was part of a much larger castle, defended by many more towers and a moat. Henry also built a new palace outside the White Tower

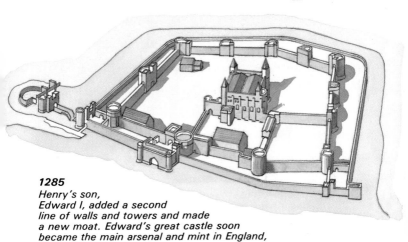

1285

Henry's son, Edward I, added a second line of walls and towers and made a new moat. Edward's great castle soon became the main arsenal and mint in England, and an important royal treasury

50

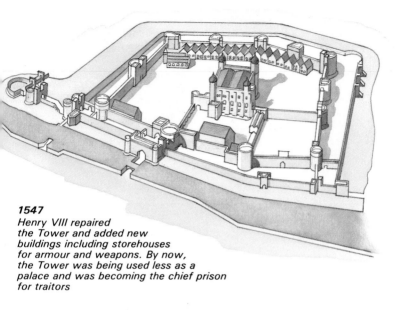

1547
Henry VIII repaired
the Tower and added new
buildings including storehouses
for armour and weapons. By now,
the Tower was being used less as a
palace and was becoming the chief prison
for traitors

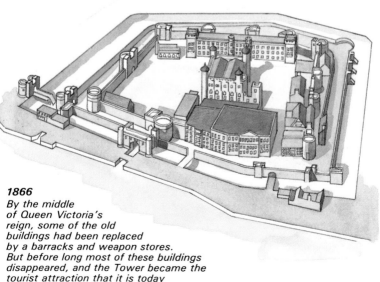

1866
By the middle
of Queen Victoria's
reign, some of the old
buildings had been replaced
by a barracks and weapon stores.
But before long most of these buildings
disappeared, and the Tower became the
tourist attraction that it is today

Index